to my little brother—
may you follow your
dreams but always find
your way back
home.

3 3113 02887 1095

random house 🏠 new york

Copyright © 2010 by Betsy E. Snyder

All rights reserved. Published in the United States by Random House Children's Books,
a division of Random House, Inc., New York.

Random House and the colophon are registered trademarks of Random House, Inc.

Visit us on the Web! www.randomhouse.com/kids

Educators and librarians, for a variety of teaching tools, visit us at
www.randomhouse.com/teachers

Library of Congress Cataloging-in-Publication Data
Snyder, Betsy E.
Sweet dreams lullaby / by Betsy Snyder.
p. cm.
ISBN 978-0-375-85852-9 (trade) — ISBN 978-0-375-95852-6 (lib. bdg.)
Summary: A young bunny goes to sleep and dreams of the soothing colors,
shapes, sights, and sounds of nature.
[1. Stories in rhyme. 2. Bedtime—Fiction. 3. Nature—Fiction. 4. Dreams—Fiction.
5. Rabbits—Fiction. 6. Lullabies.]
I. Title.
PZ8.3.S67426Sw 2010
[E]—dc22
2008052265

MANUFACTURED IN CHINA

10 9 8 7 6 5 4 3 2 1
First Edition

sweet dreams
Lullaby

betsy snyder

the day is done. it's time for bed.

let peaceful moments fill your head.

so cuddle up and snuggle in,

and let your happy dreams begin.

dream of comforts all around,

in soothing colors, shapes, and sounds.

set your cares and wishes free

to ride the dandelion breeze.

dream of eggs wrapped in a nest

where mama bird has come to rest.

imagine blossoms, soft as snow,

that blanket flower beds below.

dream of clouds like puffy pillows;

a canopy of weeping willows.

while you're lazing on your back,

dream of yummy bedtime snacks.

dream of gentle raindrop showers

giving drinks to thirsty flowers.

hummingbirds sip water up

from teeny-tiny buttercups.

dream of ducks with fluffy feathers

washing up in rainy weather.

a puddle makes a perfect bath

for little ones who like to splash.

dream of water-lily beds

where baby peepers rest their heads.

a daddy frog sings low and deep,

lulling all the pond to sleep.

dream of tiptoes through the grass

and fireflies that blink and flash,

catching night-lights floating by—

then sending them into the sky.

dream of old owl, speckled white,

who watches over all the night.

squirrels curl up, safe and snug,

while woolly bears give furry hugs.

dream of purple twilight skies,

a bedtime kiss from butterflies.

caterpillars in cocoons

are tucked in tight beneath the moon.

tiny stars are shining bright,

whispering a warm "good night."

wish on twinkles up above

and dream of everything you love.

sleep is near, so close your eyes.

drift off to this lullaby.

may Mother Nature comfort you

and make your sweetest dreams come true!

squirrel

acorn

the

bumble-
bee